William Wilkens Warren

Autobiography and Genealogy of William Wilkins Warren

William Wilkens Warren

Autobiography and Genealogy of William Wilkins Warren

ISBN/EAN: 9783337122874

Printed in Europe, USA, Canada, Australia, Japan

Cover: Foto ©Raphael Reischuk / pixelio.de

More available books at **www.hansebooks.com**

THE

AUTOBIOGRAPHY AND GENEALOGY

OF

WILLIAM WILKINS WARREN.

Printed for Family Distribution.

CAMBRIDGE:

JOHN WILSON AND SON.

University Press.

1884.

Spenser W. Richardson
with the esteem of
Wm. W. Warren

Feby 1886.

REBECCA BENNETT WARREN.

WILLIAM WILKINS WARREN

This Volume

I DEDICATE TO MY NEPHEWS AND NIECES,

FOR WHOSE USE AND BENEFIT, AND THAT OF THEIR DESCENDANTS, IT IS
SPECIALLY PREPARED AS A TOKEN OF AFFECTION.

WILLIAM WILKINS WARREN.

BOSTON, January 1, 1884.

List of Illustrations.

AUTOBIOGRAPHY.

I WAS born in Arlington (formerly West Cambridge), in a house in the centre of the town, on the main street, opposite Medford Street, as were also my three sisters. I distinctly remember the house (now still standing), with its brick ends, and a mulberry tree in front. My father's shoe-shop was close by. He and his father before him were shoemakers. My father was a quiet man, of gentle disposition and good habits, except that of extravagance. He joined the cavalry regiment raised under command of Col. Thomas Russell, his brother-in-law, about the close of the war with Great Britain. My mother had good features and figure, and was a very industrious, capable woman; or, to quote the venerable Nathan Robbins now living, "uncommonly smart and fine-looking."

About the year 1820 the financial troubles of my father were the cause of his leaving his family for New York, and my mother had to depend upon her own energies. Her daughter Frances, then four years of age, was taken by

her uncle, Col. Thomas Russell, who brought her up like
his own daughters, until her marriage with William
Schouler ; the youngest was boarded with a relative ; I
was sent to my grandfather Warren's in Medford ; and
the oldest daughter, Harriet Ann, was retained by my
mother.

While with my grandfather, who had a farm with an
orchard of about fifteen acres, I became ambitious to study
and earn money, and was careful of my earnings, which were
made in various ways, — one of which was in " sticking
cards," by putting the crooked wire-teeth through per-
forated leather for carding wool and cotton by hand-labor :
the celebrated Whittemore card-factory in West Cambridge afterwards did them with their wonderful machines.
My winter months — or those when farming was not in
progress — were devoted to study in the primary and
grammar schools, and about six months of the year to
working with my grandfather and his hired man on the
farm. I became an enthusiastic young farmer at the early
age of ten years, and so remained until I was about twelve
years old. My grandparents were very pious and kind and
affectionate to me, — my grandmother especially so. To
them I owe much for what religious traits of character
I possess. While with my grandparents, my mother, with
sister Harriet Ann removed to Medford, where she occupied the Buckman house close by. While there she was
taken into the church (now Unitarian) of Rev. Dr. Osgood
in Medford, when she and all her children were baptized. Dr. Osgood was a contemporary and friend of her
grandfather, Rev. Dr. Henry Cumings, of Billerica. Her
sister Henrietta (Aunt Cheever, now living (1883) at

the advanced age of over ninety years, was present at the ceremony.

My Sunday-school days were divided between West Cambridge (where my grandparents attended the church, now Unitarian, over which the Rev. Dr. Fisk was pastor) and Medford, where the school was under the direction of Miss Lucy Osgood, and I had Miss Elizabeth Brooks for teacher. About 1824 my mother removed to Boston, taking with her my sister Harriet Ann, and resided in a house now standing in the rear of No. 24 Myrtle Street, the first in the court, and occupied in 1883 by Mrs. Hartshorne and family.

The subsequent three years of my home with my grandparents were marked by some important events to break the monotony of my life.

The visit of General Lafayette was a great event for me, as it was to the nation. I walked alone to Charlestown, and saw on Charlestown Bridge the great procession on its way to Bunker Hill for the laying of the corner-stone of the monument.

My grandfather let a part of his house to the Reed family, one of whose members, Theresa Rebecca Reed, caused a great excitement in her escape from the Ursuline Convent in Charlestown, where she was a novice; and whose story, " Six Months in a Convent," published by a committee, was one of the causes that led to the destruction of that building by a fanatical mob. I enjoyed much the society of the Reed family, consisting of the parents and three pretty and intelligent daughters. Another daughter, Elvira, was born during their occupancy of my grandfather's house, and she is now living, —

the wife of Joseph L. Stone, a retired banker of State
Street, Boston.

The last years with my grandparents were divided between farming and attending the town school, where I was
successively under the tutelage of Mr. Furness (afterwards
Rev. Dr. Furness of Philadelphia) and Luther Angier.
During those school-days I never identified myself with
the Medford fighting-boys, who were hostile to the Charlestown boys, and had many a hard fight with them on the
frozen Middlesex Canal, then a water highway from the
Charles River to the Merrimac at Lowell. It was near
our house, and afforded me, as did the Mystic River, much
amusement in seeing the passenger and freight boats go
through the locks, and the alewife fishing in the Mystic.

About my twelfth year, at the recommendation of my
tutor, Luther Angier, who became a lifelong friend, I was
taken into the family of John Angier, who kept the Academy
at Medford, — a brother of Luther, Charles, and Joseph.
The last two became Unitarian ministers. There I had all
the benefits of that excellent institution, my tuition being
paid in work in and about the premises. The principal and
his housekeeper, Miss Betsy Kuhn, took a lively interest in
my welfare, and our friendly relations were kept up in after
years during their whole lives. There were many gradu-
ates of this Academy who became distinguished as mer-
chants of long-standing. At the annual exhibition I had a
part assigned to me in declamation, and I had commenced
studying French just before leaving for Boston in 1828.

Soon after I came to Mr. Angier's (1820) my mother was
married in May of that year to Capt. Joseph Attwood of the
Merchant Marine Service. Meantime, Russell Smith,

widower at twenty-one years of age, who had met my sister Harriet Ann at his jewelry store, proposed marriage to her about two years after their meeting. She was very fond of music, and became a proficient on the piano and in singing before her marriage, which took place in the autumn of 1826, at which I was present with others of the family, —among them my aged aunt before mentioned. Father Ballou performed the ceremony at my mother's home.

In November following, Captain Attwood with his wife, and sister Harriet Ann and her husband, sailed for St. Thomas, W. I., to take up their residence there. Captain Attwood had abandoned his profession, and took with him furniture and wares to open an American hotel. The great change of climate and imprudent exertion of my mother produced yellow fever, of which she died Jan. 28, 1827, at the early age of thirty-five. Captain Attwood returned home soon after selling out, and died in June following. Mr. Smith established a jewelry and fancy-goods store, which afterwards became a prominent establishment.

In 1828, at the age of fourteen, I left of my own choice the Academy, to learn the trade of a printer with John B. Russell. I had read the Life of Benjamin Franklin, and took quite a fancy for that mechanical art, in which he was so distinguished a workman. Moreover, Mr. Russell was a nephew of my Uncle Russell, and offered me such inducements and preferment as compensated me for leaving the Academy before graduating. Mr. Russell was the proprietor, printer, and publisher of the "New England Farmer," edited by Thomas Green Fessenden, an accomplished writer and poet. In Mr. Russell's family I found kind friends and a happy home. A close and firm friend-

ship was established between us at that time, which has
been maintained ever since; and to this day his gentle,
genial, and most estimable qualities are enjoyed by myself
and those who know him as intimately as I do. He is
over eighty-two years of age, and yet his pen shows the
vigor of a man in prime of life. Yet, as he recently wrote
me, "the premonitions of the great final change I meet
with satisfaction and real pleasure."

During my apprenticeship I was at once promoted to
the "galleys," — that is, to type-setting. As a compositor,
I had to stand on a box to reach the "cases," not having
attained my growth. I also tried my hand a little at
proof-reading. After a year thus employed, Mr. Russell
relinquished printing to establish the first seed-establish-
ment in Boston, and was the founder of that now kept by
Breck & Son, in North-Market Street. The publication
of the "Farmer" he still retained. His proposition to me
to remain with him in the new enterprise was accepted, and
I became a general-utility boy; keeping the "Farmer"
ledger, putting up and selling seeds, roots, and plants, and
thus making the acquaintance of eminent men interested
in agriculture and horticulture: more especially so, as the
Massachusetts Horticultural Society, in the formation of
which Mr. Russell was instrumental, had its first meet-
ings and exhibitions in the large room over the seed-store.
In its history I am credited with being its first librarian.
I enjoyed the exhibitions much, and became quite a judge
of flowers and fruit, especially the latter, when the exhibitions were over. I remember the first annual dinner of
the Society which I was admitted to, at which time I made
my first acquaintance with champagne, and heard that

wonderfully gifted comic actor and poet Henry J. Finn, who sang a comic song on the occasion.

While thus enjoying my situation with Mr. Russell, I received an offer from Mr. Smith at St. Thomas to come there, with funds for the voyage. I felt at a loss what to do. I wished to be with my sister and see the little world at St. Thomas, and a tropical life was tempting. I consulted my best friend, Mr. Russell, for advice. His interest, he said, was to retain me ; but my interest was to embrace the offer, which opened a better field for advancement than he could promise me. His views coincided with my own ; and investing my spare money in Lewis's famous tomato ketchup, and with a consignment of seeds from Mr. Russell, I left in November in the brig "Odessa" for St. Thomas, with several other passengers. Capt. John Winship of the Brighton Nurseries, with whom I was a favorite, sent on board a barrel of apples, and at parting, with a hearty slap on the shoulder, said, " Willie, my boy, always remember to look after No. 1 ! "

I enjoyed the voyage without any sea-sickness ; and the group of islands rising like mountains out of the blue waters of the Caribbean Sea, through which we sailed, was a new and wonderful sight, while the fresh green tropical clothing of Nature was in strong contrast to the snowy and wintry one left behind. How much greater my pleasure at meeting my sister and her husband, may be imagined ! Everything was so novel. The city built on three hills, backed by steep mountains ; its beautiful land-locked harbor, with a hundred ships of different nations ; the slave domestics at the houses, so different in looks and manner from what I expected, — all combined to give a wonderful

pleasure not excelled in all my after travels. I was speedily
introduced into society, and found many warm friends
among the foreigners who frequented our house. There
were only a half-dozen American families residing there,
the population of ten thousand being made up, exclusive
of slaves and free-colored, of different European nations,
engaged principally in mercantile business, there not being
much sugar or other West-India product raised on the
island. It is a free port, and an *entrepôt* for goods which
are purchased there to go to other islands, and transshipped
in small vessels. The best and well cultivated families
lived in luxury and comfort, and were remarkably social and
hospitable, fond of music, dancing, giving parties, and keeping open-house for visitors to drop in, and welcomed without ceremony. The Danish governor, military and naval
officers, and city officials were more exclusive, but appeared
frequently at balls and parties. At the time of which I
write, slavery existed in the Danish islands of St. Thomas,
St. Croix or Santa Cruz, and St. John. All males above
sixteen years were obliged to do militia duty, though there
was a garrison of regular troops. The climate is such that
linen suits and straw hats are worn all the year round
during the day, and the temperature never falls in winter
below 65° at night, the average being 70° in winter and 75°
in summer. My enjoyment of the society into which I
was thrown, was beyond all my anticipation. The prominent vices, especially drinking and gambling, which pre-
vailed among all classes, I avoided during my ten years'
residence there, by studiously keeping the good resolution
I made on my arrival. Tobacco, smoked so universally,
is a stranger to my lips. I however became excessively

fond of music and dancing, which there were daily op-
portunities to enjoy the year round ; and the many lady
friends of my sister gave me congenial enjoyment of
female society, which did much to keep me from that of
my male friends and their vices. I could fill a volume with
details of life in St. Thomas of much interest, but will only
introduce into my brief narrative a few episodes.

I soon at Mr. Smith's store learned the business ; and
our trade being in part with Spaniards from off the island,
I learned something of their language. French and German, though spoken all around me, I never attempted to
learn, for the speakers mostly knew English. I learned
the sounds of the words, which with the knowledge of
the manners and customs of the different nations was a
valuable acquisition to me in my after travels in Europe.

The year after my arrival I wrote a description of St.
Thomas, — its inhabitants, commerce, and its fruits and
vegetables. I sent the same to John B. Russell, and he
published *verbatim* my description of the fruits and vegetables, which occupied two columns of the " New England
Farmer" of Oct. 5, 1831.

The first event of importance to me was a serious fit
of sickness (the climate fever), of long continuance, during which I was under the care of a Scotch doctor of
the " old school," who made an apothecary shop of me.
I seemed to linger without any improvement, when our
landlord, a country planter, said to Mr. Smith, " That
boy will die unless you get him away from physic and
bad air," — at the same time offering his house, and
negro slaves to take me to it. I was put upon a mule's
back, sustained there by two negroes, and conveyed to

his estate three miles distant, a thousand feet above the
sea. The attentive care of me by his wife and daughters,
and the country diet and fresh air, wrought a speedy
cure. There being no carriage roads in the country,
except a mile or two at either end of the town, and the
hills being steep, horseback riding was a frequent enjoyment in the early morning or evening, to avoid the tropical heat. This was mitigated, however, by the trade-wind,
which sets in each forenoon. Stormy days are unknown ;
and showers, which come and go suddenly, give all the
rainfall necessary to supply the cisterns for family use
and drink.

Soon after my arrival Mr. Smith commenced building a
pretty and commodious house on the top of one of the
hills overlooking the harbor, with its front standing on
the edge of a precipice of rock, and looking down upon the
red-tiled roofs of the houses. Soon after my recovery we
moved into it, and I had the American flag displayed from
a staff on the battlement-wall supporting the gallery of the
house in front.

On the 31st day of January, 1832, at midnight, a fire
broke out in the city. The fort fired the signal guns,
the drums of the fire-corps were beat through the streets,
and the bacchanalian pleasures of the New Year, rife at
that hour, ceased ; but the rapid spread of the flames defied
all attempts to check it. The fire continued to burn in the
business and most valued portion of the town (mostly built
of fire-proof material) all the next day, destroying over a
thousand buildings, with a loss computed at eight million
dollars. A heavy shower, and a canal intersecting the city,
put a stop to the flames. Our store was of one high story,

with flat roof covered with tiles set in cement, and large, wooden folding-doors covered with sheet-iron. With the aid of six lumber-yard negroes, belonging in part to Mr. Smith, we worked all night, removing goods on board a vessel in the harbor. The flames were close upon us when all but a piano was removed ; and, shutting the ponderous, high doors, we left the building to burn. But it fortunately escaped the terrible heat of the flames in its rear.

Mr. Smith had entered into a copartnership with Christian Dickmann, a Swede and neighbor, for the sale of lumber ; and in the spring of 1833 he proposed my going to the States to purchase goods and see my family, — offering on my return to give me a home and one thousand dollars a year salary ; or, at my option, to take me as a partner, he putting in as capital the stock of goods, and giving me one half the net profits. I chose the latter ; and visited the cities of Philadelphia, New York, and Boston, making purchases, and having considerable time during six months' absence to enjoy my first travels as well as the family and friends at home in West Cambridge.

On the first day of January, 1834, at the age of nineteen, I entered on our copartnership, the papers of which I drew up, and have now in my possession. I soon had nearly the whole management of the store, owing to Mr. Smith's occupation in other business. Our book-keeper had taught me double-entry book-keeping, and I was assisted by a slave belonging to Mr. Smith, and a boy belonging to the firm.

Soon after, Mr. Smith visited the States to purchase goods. During his absence I hired the adjoining store, fitted both up in one with handsome fixtures, and greatly increased the business and profits. On his return, Mr.

Smith expressed himself as well pleased with my judgment and management; and having received a cargo of lumber in a brig, for which he desired to furnish a return freight, he sent me over to Santa Cruz in her for a cargo of sugar and molasses, which I obtained.

In the spring of 1835 I again visited the States, as a naturalized Danish citizen, having to become so to do business in the colony. During my visit I became acquainted with my future wife, through my sister Sarah, her mutual and intimate friend. I also made the very pleasant acquaintance of William Schouler, who was engaged to my sister Frances. He was with his father and elder brother in the print-works, established by them in West Cambridge. An account of his family will be found hereafter in the Schouler genealogy. Mr. Schouler and my sister were married at Col. Thomas Russell's, Oct. 6, 1835, before I left for New York. While awaiting the sailing of the vessel for St. Thomas, at New York, the great fire of November took place; and I witnessed the devastation of a large territory in and around Wall Street, the like of which is only exceeded by that of Chicago and Boston. A great conflagration in the metropolis of the United States is yet in the future, perhaps not far distant.

The spring of 1836 found me for the first time keeping bachelor's hall in Mr. Smith's house, he having gone with my sister to the United States to purchase goods, giving her the first opportunity to revisit home and our dear sisters and other relatives in West Cambridge. I had with me all Mr. Smith's slave domestics, four in number, besides as many of their children. While living thus, taking my meals at the hotel, my friend, Thomas Messenger, a

merchant of New York, afterwards a noted and valuable citizen of Brooklyn, visited me, which led to another life-long friendship.

Mr. Smith and sister Harriet Ann returned late in the autumn with sister Sarah. Her visit was a very delightful episode in our life. Santa Cruz was visited, and the beautiful drives and the social parties of this lovely island were a new delight to us. I looked forward to my visit in 1837 with great interest, as my marriage was then to take place. In May of that year I went home with sister Sarah in a ship to New York, on which we had a most enjoyable voyage. My meeting those most dear to me may be imagined. Many happy days were spent in West Cambridge, at the house of my brother-in-law William Schouler, who had become a political writer; and frequent were my visits to Billerica, driving over the Middlesex Turnpike with a horse and chaise which I had purchased. My marriage day was a beautiful one in autumn, the 17th of October; and the house of Joshua Bennett, of Billerica, at noon, was well filled with friends to witness the ceremony. After its close, and dinner over, a final leave was taken, for we were to go to New York to embark for our home in St. Thomas. The carriage of my wife's father conveyed us to Boston, where we stopped over night at the Marlboro' Hotel, going thence the next day to New York. We were most hospitably received at the house of Colonel Barrett on Staten Island, whose wife and family — aunt and cousins of my wife Rebecca — made our stay of a few days exceedingly enjoyable.

Our first voyage together made to St. Thomas was in the ship "Whitmore," which took out a number of distin-

guished passengers. We started in a severe gale of wind
from the northeast, which lasted three days. We ran before it with a single sail, had our decks swept by heavy
seas, and made the passage in nine days. During my
absence a terrible hurricane had visited the island. Trees
were uprooted, many buildings were demolished, and most
of the vessels in the harbor were either sunk at their
anchors or driven ashore.

Our arrival was welcomed by Mr. Smith, my sister, and
a host of friends; and society with its numerous parties
and balls was very gay, and quite in contrast to American life at home. I took out with us a carriage, and purchased a fine horse in Santa Cruz, as also a pony for my wife
to ride. It is difficult to convey an adequate idea of the
pleasures enjoyed in our island home. The winter months
soon passed; but Mr. Smith, who was suffering from a
pulmonary disease, made a visit to the Dutch Island of
Curaçoa to get relief.

In the spring of 1858 he again with his wife left for the
States to purchase goods as before, but never to return;
for after trying the Thomsonian Infirmary in Boston he
failed rapidly, and died suddenly October 18, just after
purchasing goods from Bigelow Brothers. His loss was
keenly felt by us all, — by none more than myself; for
his generosity and kindness had advanced me rapidly in
business and fortune. Leaving no will to save his estate
from passing into the hands of the Danish Probate Court
for a disadvantageous settlement, I effected a compromise
with the judge, who allowed me, on payment of a large fee
into the court treasury, to have the sole settlement of the
estate, both real and personal, without bonds. A required

VIEW OF ST. THOMAS, WEST INDIES

power of attorney from the heirs-at-law was obtained, and
the estate was finally settled on my return to Boston in
1839. The settlement included the sale of Mr. Smith's
house and furniture, domestic and other slaves, and the
lumber-yard lot of land, — his partner, Mr. Dickmann,
having died before him.

Leaving my business with my principal clerk and sales-
man, with a power of attorney, and Mr. Francis Kemlo of
Boston in the watch-repairing department, I again visited
the States, taking my wife with me, in the spring of 1839,
with the determination of closing up my business on our
return. In company with my wife's sister Ellen we made a
very pleasant tour in the summer, going as far west as Pitts-
burg, Pa., travelling from the lakes to that city by stage.
After a very pleasant visit, we left on our return to St.
Thomas by way of New York. It was on our passage
from Stonington to the latter city that we experienced the
most critical danger of our lives in travelling. The frail
but swift steamer "Lexington," whose terrible fate afterwards by fire is still well remembered, left Stonington in
a gale, which increased in two hours to a hurricane. Being built for speed, of great length and narrow beam, she
was unable to cope with the heavy seas. Her decks were
swept, the water flooded the berth deck; baggage was
taken from the crates and distributed to trim the vessel;
every sea that broke over her quarter threatened to swamp
her; she was put off her course before the wind; passengers were grouped about in despair; a driving mist blinded
our course. I found my trunk, and from it took two life-
preservers, which I had designed for use in St. Thomas
as swimming-belts, rigged cords to them, and prepared

for the worst. Most providentially, about midnight the tempest lulled and the mist parted, revealing to us the horror that we were driving towards Long Island. The lull enabled us to change our course, and escape from another peril. We embarked in the ship "Camilla" for St. Thomas, and had a pleasant passage. Among the passengers was the Rev. John Joseph Gurney, the celebrated Quaker scholar and philanthropist, proposing a tour through the West Indies, who afterwards, in his book describing his travels, gave a true account of the condition of slavery there. We enjoyed his friendship on and after the voyage.

The spring of 1840 in St. Thomas I devoted to closing out the stock of goods by private sale, and finally by auction held for several days at the store. Having realized cash for most of the goods, leaving what was due me to be collected by my attorney, I returned to Boston with my wife in May, 1840. I left the store in possession of Messrs. Kemlo & Mitchell, my employees, who purchased the fixtures to establish the same business, and who were subsequently joined by Alexander Aitken, a Scotch jeweller, who was afterwards lost on his return from Europe with all his goods purchased there. This disaster soon caused the failure of the new enterprise.

My limits will not allow me to dwell on the subsequent events of my life, and therefore I shall briefly advert to some of the most prominent, though they all are more or less familiar to our own families.

Soon after our return I purchased from my brother-in-law, William Schouler, a five-acre lot bordering on Spy Pond in West Cambridge. This was laid out on a plan

I had drawn while at sea; a Doric villa was erected and hundreds of trees and shrubs set out the same year, the whole being completed so that we were in full enjoyment of it the spring following. The place was much admired, and from its novel construction was called the West-India House. While here I became interested in the great political campaign of 1840, which resulted in Whig supremacy and the overthrow of the Jackson policy. The great Washingtonian movement and temperance revival also had my earnest support. About this time I became interested in the initial steps for a railroad, taking part in the survey, and being counsel for the petitioners before the legislative committee, which resulted in the bill granted for the Lexington and West Cambridge Railroad. The subject of mesmerism, then coming prominently before the public, claimed much of my attention, and I succeeded in mesmerizing several persons, among others the god-child of my sister, Harriet Ann Dickmann, from St. Thomas, then residing with us. In September, 1840, my sister, Mrs. Smith, was married to George M. Chalwill of St. Thomas, who took up his residence in Boston. The following spring my wife's sister Ellen was married to George Holden. In 1842 my youngest sister Sarah married Oliver W. Blake.

From 1840 to 1845, no desirable opportunity presenting itself to me for engaging in such a business as I wished to follow, I assisted my father-in-law in the management and care of his real estate in Lowell and Boston, and of his other business of buying and selling hops, which was of considerable magnitude.

In 1846 an opportunity was offered to me to embark in a business congenial to my taste and with which I was

familiar. William W. Messer, who had been brought up
in it by a firm with which I had done business while in
St. Thomas, proposed forming a copartnership, and estab-
lishing in Boston the first house for importing direct from
the manufacturers in Europe the richest articles of taste
and luxury for the drawing-room and toilet, both useful and
ornamental. I accepted, and a store (No. 27 Kilby Street)
was hired, and Mr. Messer left for Europe to purchase a
stock and open relations with the manufacturers through
commission houses in England and the continent.

Meantime I sold my beautiful estate on Spy Pond, with
all my furniture, for cash, without a loss on the real estate,
which afterward nearly doubled in value within ten years.
The proceeds were used in our business; and in three years
the profits about doubled our capital. In 1847 I succeeded
Mr. Messer in going to Europe to buy goods, and took my
wife with me on our first visit there. We sailed from New
York in a Havre packet, and had a voyage of twenty-eight
days. Ernest Evers, a German, engaged to act as our
agent on a salary, accompanied us, and was established in
our warehouse in Paris for purchasing and shipping, — thus
saving commissions, and giving us advantages with the
manufacturers. During our absence of eight months we
travelled extensively over Europe, and I wrote a series of
letters for the "Boston Atlas," edited by William Schouler.
There I became acquainted with Spiridion, the Paris cor-
respondent of that paper, and a friendship of many years
resulted therefrom. In 1846 we removed to Boston, boarding on Somerset Street with Mrs. Prescott, and in the
winter of 1847 we commenced boarding with Mrs. Slater,
8 Allston Street. In 1848 our business increased rapidly.

HARRIET, FRANCES, AND SARAH

Being untrammelled by business, which had been satis-
factorily settled up, I had my whole time for enjoyment.
Ireland and Scotland were visited for the first time, and a
winter spent in Paris. While travelling in the South of
France, a serious accident in a diligence prevented our going
to Spain ; and after our return to Paris, accompanied by
Dr. H. Richardson, I visited the Crimea, just before the
close of the war, and wrote letters from there to the "Boston
Atlas." My wife, with Miss Richardson and the Davenports,
remained, during our absence, in Paris. We visited Malta,
Athens, Smyrna, and Constantinople *en route* to Sebastopol.
After our return, our party were honored by invitations to
the grand ball at the Hotel de Ville, given by the City of
Paris to King Victor Emanuel, — one of the most splendid
ever given. Our Minister had only seventy-five admissions
allotted to the United States, of which we had five. The
first Great World's Exposition, which took place in Paris,
in the Bois de Boulogne, was visited before our return in the
summer of 1856. Another important event which occurred
during our stay in Paris was the birth of the Prince Impe-
rial, which was hailed with great joy, and Eugenie became
idolized.

After our return, I entered into an arrangement with my
father-in-law to take the entire charge of his real-estate in
Boston and Lowell, and employed as my collector W. S. Kyle,
with an office on State Street. The same year, having purchased the large estate No. 8 Allston Street, I remodelled
the house, building another in the rear, and reserving a
suite on the first floor for our permanent home, where we
had already been boarding with Mrs. Slater ten years. In
the winter I was seized with a violent attack of inflamma-

tory rheumatism. After many weeks of suffering I was, with the aid of my good nurse Susan Stetson, able to start in April for the South with my wife, and from New Orleans went up the Mississippi to St. Paul, where the extreme heat of that city in July effaced all remains of my malady. Miss Davenport, meanwhile, having purchased an estate on Ocean Street, Lynn, I was induced to buy two estates adjoining hers only by the division of King Street. Extensive alterations were made, — one house moved away; the two lots thrown together, — and we moved in and recommenced housekeeping in Bellevue Cottage after an interval of eleven years. Here we spent about six months of the year, living during the other six at our pleasant home on Allston Street. Mr. Bennett had removed to Boston, having purchased a house on Chamber Street, which was fitted up by me for his use in winter months. During the next four years the great financial crisis of 1859 affected my investments in St. Paul, which was the occasion of my making many visits there, in order to look after the security of my property. I also added to my Lynn estate, including the cottage named for my brother-in-law, General Schouler, who occupied it for many years, both before and after the War of the Rebellion.

While visiting Nuremberg in 1856, the Schwarz Lava Gas-tip was put into my hands exclusively for its introduction into the United States, and a patent was obtained for it in Washington. The merits of it, and the success of the sales, soon brought forth an inferior article, and the interference case under the patent which I brought at Washington was decided in favor of Mr. Schwarz by the department there. I had the monopoly of the sales in the

United States for many years at a large profit. At present the article is universally used at a low cost, the patent having expired.

At the breaking out of the Great Rebellion in April, 1861, I assisted Adjutant-General Schouler in getting off the first Massachusetts regiments, and gave my time for several weeks in his department, — a service handsomely acknowledged by Governor Andrew in his message. In 1862, just before the municipal election, I was solicited to be a candidate for the Common Council in Ward 4 (now 10), and was elected a member for that year and the two succeeding years. My duties were arduous, being appointed to serve on five important committees, — Public Buildings, Accounts, Harbor, Relief, and Recruiting. The building of the City Hall, and its furnishing, received much attention from me as one of the sub-committee, and the laying out of its space in front as well as the pattern of its fence were after my own designs.

The last year of my service in the Council was an important one. And here I must relate one of the most critical portions of my life, which occurred in April, 1865. While in my rooms at Allston Street on a Sunday morning, reading the paper, I was suddenly seized with a most severe pain in my bowels, caused by a stoppage in one of the small intestines near the stomach. It continued over three days and three nights without relief from two physicians; and then, when my life was despaired of, Dr. Morrill Wyman of Cambridge was sent for. He came on the evening of the third day, and immediately relieved me by an injection of air. I was attended in my slow recovery by Dr. Townsend, and soon after removed to

WILLIAM WILKINS WARREN AND WIFE.

my cottage in Lynn, where my father-in-law came to visit
us for the last time. He complained so much and appeared
so ill that I took him to Dr. Wyman, for examination,
who pronounced his case incurable, being Bright's disease
of the kidneys. At Billerica I was with him during most
of the last month of his sufferings, until the day of his
death, the 6th of August; and at his request made an
inventory of his property and a draft of his will in the
presence of his wife and mine. He was unable to sign it,
but it was carried out to the letter by agreement of the
heirs; and my brother-in-law, George Holden, and myself
were appointed administrators by the court. Within a year
the personal property was divided between the heirs, the
real being held undivided, and all legacies and debts paid.

My multifarious cares and steady application to business
determined me to decline further municipal honors, and
to take a long respite from business, which my impaired
health demanded.

In the early part of 1866, with my wife, her mother, and
a mutual friend, Miss Hannah P. Taylor, I took steamer
for Savannah, where we spent some weeks, and a series of
letters was there written by me, and published in the
"Boston Transcript." On our return I prepared for a two-
years' travel abroad, selling my furniture on Allston Street
and letting my cottage at the seashore.

We left in the autumn of 1866, and in Paris joined our
friends Dr. Horace Richardson, his sister Elizabeth, and
Mr. and Mrs. Charles H. Lord of Newton, all of whom
were old companions in European travel. Here was
planned our voyage up the Nile and our travels in the
Holy Land, which afterwards resulted so successfully.

giving to us all enjoyment beyond our most sanguine
expectations. The next year being that of the second
Great Exposition in the Champ de Mars in Paris, I took
the lease in that city for a year of a large *appartement* of
seven rooms, all furnished ready for housekeeping, the
rent being seven thousand francs. Gen. C. B. Norton (late
of the Foreign Exhibition in Boston), a Paris banker, let it
for me for the six months we proposed to be absent. We
left Paris in November for Marseilles, thence to Egypt, and
afterwards to the Holy Land and Syria.

Our travels and voyages in the East are fully described
in the letters I wrote for the Boston "Traveller," and which
were printed in 1867, 1873, and 1883 in book form, with the
title of "Life on the Nile, and a tour in Syria and Pales-
tine." After visiting Constantinople and Italy, we arrived
in Paris soon after the Exposition was opened, and occupied our apartments on the Rue Fauxbourg St. Honoré.
While in Egypt I received a commission from the Governor
of Massachusetts as Assistant Commissioner to the Exposition, but did not qualify myself or act, preferring to be free
from all care of any kind, that I might the better enjoy my
travels and promote my health. After seeing the World's
Fair for two months, my wife and I travelled in Denmark,
Sweden, and Russia, returning to Paris to enjoy the Exposition at its close in November. We then parted with
our Nile friends, and I having contracted a severe cold in
Paris, we visited the south of France, spending some
months in Nice, where we were joined by Dr. Richardson
and his sister.

The winter of 1867-68 in Nice was a very gay one to us.
A grand reception and ball was given by the Americans

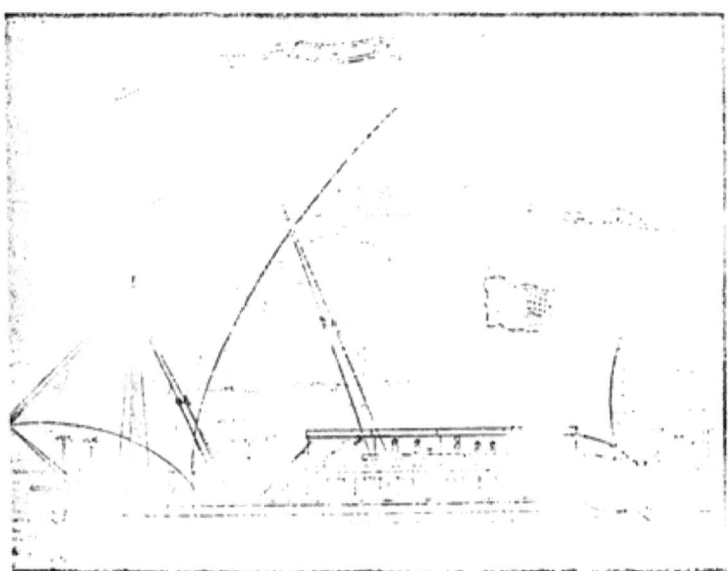

THE IRON DAHABIEH "GAZELLE" ON THE NILE.

Her dimensions are 75 feet in length from bow to stern, and 10½ in breadth. She draws 33 inches of water; the cabin floor is sunk 28 inches below the forward deck; the inwale is 10 inches above the deck, and 28 inches out of water. The height of the cabin 6½ feet. The upper deck is furnished with divans and awnings.

Bed		Bed	Divan.		Deck for 10 Sailors, Capt. Steersman, Boy, 2 Cooks, 3 Waiters and Dragoman.
Bath			
After Saloon	Passage	Saloon	
Bed	Bed	Bed	Divan.	

there to Admiral Farragut, who visited Nice with his fleet
I served on the most important of the committees. Next
to that given in Paris to the King of Italy, this ball was
the most brilliant I ever witnessed. John Schouler, my
nephew, was a lieutenant with Farragut's fleet. We had
previously met Lieutenant Schouler at Naples and St.
Petersburg.

Leaving our friends at Nice, we went to Marseilles and
crossed the Mediterranean to Algiers, which we found a
very beautiful city, and highly enjoyed it. While there a
ball was given by Marshal McMahon, afterwards President
of the French Republic, which we attended. Some letters
I wrote there were published in a Boston paper. Returning to France, we met by appointment the Richardsons at
Marseilles, and made together a tour through Spain, Por-
tugal, and the south of France. We witnessed the carnival
at Barcelona, Holy Week and Fair at Seville, and the bull-
fights in Seville and Lisbon. Gibraltar was visited en route
from Malaga to the Tagus and Lisbon. A carriage-tour
among the Pyrenees and their celebrated Baths was made
on our way back to Paris. Leaving our friends, we travelled
through England again, making a visit to a friend by invitation in Scotland, from whence by Liverpool we returned
home after two years' absence.

In the autumn of 1868 we took rooms at the St. James
Hotel, in the south part of Boston, having my wife's mother
with us, and remained there two winters. The year after
the opening of the Pacific Railroad we made, with our old
companions the Richardsons, a trip to California, visiting
the coast towns, Los Angeles, the interior valleys, the
Geysers, the Yosemite Valley, the big trees, Lake Tahoe,

and Salt Lake City. On our return we took a lease of four years of a spacious suite of rooms at the Commonwealth Hotel, where we enjoyed its society until we finally left in 1873 for Europe. The year 1872 removed from us by death our beloved William Schouler and Eben C. Haraden, both so universally esteemed. Their deaths were the first in order of eight others of our relatives to the present time of writing (1883). While at the Commonwealth occurred the great fire of November 9 and 10, 1872, which desolated so valuable a part of Boston. At its commencement I went to 25 Kilby Street, and with the help of a laborer worked all night packing and sending off to a place of safety, books, papers, and things of value stored there, feeling confident by morning the flames would reach that place. I was the last to quit the building, but the fire was arrested at its walls, and only a small amount of damage was done by the expiring flames.

The World's Fair at Vienna attracted us again to Europe in 1873. We embarked in May, at New York, in a French steamer for France, arriving in Paris from Brest, where we remained until June, when we visited Brussels, Cologne, and thence ascended the Rhine, visiting its towns again, and at Wiesbaden saw the Shah of Persia. From Basle, Switzerland, we went to Geneva, and on its lake met our old friends the Richardsons, and Peter L. Cox and family of Lynn. Thence we went to Zurich, Schaffhausen, and Munich. We finally reached Vienna by rail, and the Danube by the first of July, — it being our fourth visit since our first in 1847. During half the month we devoted ourselves to seeing the Great World's Fair, greater in extent than any of its predecessors, and then left for a tour through

Austria, Switzerland, and Germany, to return again. Ischel was again enjoyed, and the fine carriage-drive to Salzburg by the lovely lakes. Thence to Innsbruck among the Austrian Alps, where we met Mr. and Mrs. Cox, and with them took the carriage journey through the Engadine to Samaden and St. Moritz in Switzerland. Here our friends left, and we journeyed on alone by the Albula Pass to Coire. Thence by rail to Lucerne, and steamer and carriage to Flüelen, St. Gothard, and Andermatt; thence by carriage to Glacier du Rhone, Zermatt (where we ascended the Gorner Gratt, ten thousand three hundred feet above sea level), Leukerbad, at the Gemmi Pass, to Vevay. We visited Geneva again, meeting friends there who travelled with us to Berne, Interlachen, Basle, Strasburg, Baden Baden, Kissengen, Dresden, and Leipsic. Thence we proceeded alone to Teplitz, and arrived at Prague, where my wife was ill some days. We next left for Vienna, arriving September 11, where we met Dr. Richardson and sister, besides many other friends, visiting the Exposition. The King of Italy, Victor Emmanuel, was visiting Vienna, and had a grand reception. It was my good fortune to be for two hours with his party of fifty, including the Emperor and suite, at the great Horse Exhibition, in the Annex.

With the Richardsons we made a trip down the Danube to Buda-Pest, in Hungary, returning to Vienna by rail, where we finished our purchases at the exhibition. Bid adieu to friends, and left for Italy by the Simmering Pass, Gratz, and Trieste. After visiting the home of Maximilian, Miramar, we left for Venice, where we met friends and enjoyed our visit there much. From Venice we went to Verona, Milan, Genoa, and arrived at Nice to spend the

winter there November 1. Here we met the Richardsons again.

After a delightful four months spent at Nice, we left with our friends for a trip to the island of Corsica, — to Bastia by steamer, and by carriage across the island over mountains to Ajaccio, the beautiful native city of Napoleon I. Returning as we came, and nearly snowed up in the mountains, we embarked at Bastia for Leghorn, thence to Rome and Naples. While at the latter place I made a trip to the Island of Sicily alone, visiting Palermo, Messina, Catania, at the foot of Mt. Etna, and Syracuse. Returning to Naples, after again seeing Sorrento, Pompeii, and the blue grotto, we left for the Italian lakes, and thence to Turin, and by the St. Cenis tunnel to Paris, leaving our friends in Italy. Spending some weeks in Paris, we left for England, and after a week in London departed for Liverpool, where we embarked on board the steamer "Siberia" for Boston the 9th of June. With a broken propeller on this old Cunarder, our voyage of twelve days was not a very pleasant one; but our whole European tour of fourteen months proved very enjoyable and fortunate.

Three days after our arrival, James Schouler left to join his wife in Europe. After a month spent in Billerica, we went to Lynn for the summer with sister Sarah. Emma, and Henry, at the Bellevue. At this time I built upon the estate on the corner of Ocean and King streets, which I had purchased during my absence, and gave some five months to this work. Two Indian skeletons were unearthed in digging for a cellar. King Street was narrowed ten feet, and that strip enclosed in my estates. We took a trip to Saratoga, and visited sister Frances at her son

William's in Syracuse. We returned to Billerica, sister Harriet with Mrs. Calef then boarding there. October 31, learning that my dear sister Frances was in a critical state of fever, I left that night, arriving at Syracuse in the morning to find her departed. She was buried on the 4th of November, sister Harriet going for the last time to Boston to attend the funeral.

On the 9th we took up our quarters for the winter at the Revere House, and mother joined us two weeks after. Little Willie Schouler was buried the next day. The events of the winter were the visit of King Kalakua, and my meeting him at a Masonic banquet; the marriage of Hattie Schouler in Boston, which sister Harriet Ann at North Reading was not able to attend; the visit of General Grant to Boston, and the great Centennial Celebration at Lexington, April 19, 1875.

Soon after, we left the Revere and went to Billerica, remaining till the 10th of June, when we resumed housekeeping in the Bellevue at Lynn, having had new improvements made. Sister Sarah, Emma, and Henry were also with us; sister Harriet made us her last visit. On the 17th of August our pleasant summer was clouded over by the death of Rebecca Holden, universally beloved. We left September 20 for Billerica, and afterwards visited New York.

On the 26th of October we left Billerica for our large suite of rooms at Mrs. Anabel's, No. 11 Beacon Street, which was to be our pleasant home for several years, with mother most of the time with us. The winter passed pleasantly, varied by duties at the Franklin Savings-Bank, Washingtonian Home, and attendance at the Art

Club.   On the 6th of February, 1876, George Holden died
after a long illness, soon following his daughter Rebecca.
During the spring I had a rheumatic attack.   On the 17th
of April we left with Miss Taylor for a visit to Philadelphia
and the Centennial.   The Emperor and Empress of Brazil
were at our Hotel in Philadelphia, and I had the honor
of an introduction to the Empress.   We witnessed the
opening of the Centennial World's Exhibition, and remained two weeks to see it.   We next went to Washington, and thence returned home to Boston; afterwards
to Billerica, and then spent a month at Princeton, where
we were joined by mother and Ellen; thence we returned
to Billerica, just before the decease of Aunt Mary Rand,
August 13.   On the 30th following, sister Harriet Ann
had a stroke of paralysis, depriving her of speech for a
while.   I attended the breaking of ground for the unfortu-
nate narrow (twelve-inch) gauge railroad for Bedford and
Billerica, September 6.   On the 20th we left for Philadelphia with mother, Ellen, and Emma to visit the Exposition.
Mrs. Lander and Dr. Richardson and sister arrived later
at the United States Hotel, near the Centennial grounds.
After two weeks we went to New York, and home again.
The election for President produced immense excitement,
— Tilden against Hayes; and the election left in doubt.
We spent three weeks at the Tremont House, having
rented our rooms for the winter to go South.

   We left November 27 for Washington, where we spent
Thanksgiving week, and then left for Jacksonville, Florida.
We made an excursion up the River St. John and back in
December, and were joined by our nieces, the Richard-
sons, and Mrs. Dr. Ball, to visit the West India Islands.

James Schouler and wife were met at Jacksonville, who also were on a Florida tour.   **1927805**

Jan. 3, 1877, of a frosty morning, our party of five left in the train for Cedar Keys, on the Gulf of Mexico, where we awaited the arrival of the steamer from New Orleans that touched outside the bar on her way to Havana. Our voyage in the "Tappahannock" was varied by the stop for some hours at Key West, and on the fourth day we anchored in the fine harbor of Havana. We spent ten days there, during which we made an excursion to Matanzas and its beautiful cave by the sea. On the 23d we embarked on the fine ocean steamer, the "Ville de Nazaire" of the French trans-atlantic line, bound for Martinique, and thence home to France. Our voyage was a most delightful one to Mar-tinique, along the islands of Cuba, St. Domingo, and Porto Rico, arriving at my former island home, St. Thomas, where we stopped a day; thence by the group of the Virgin Islands, to the eastern group of the Antilles. We touched at Guadaloupe, and arrived on the sixth day at our destination, the lovely tropical island of Martinique. While there we visited the birthplace of Josephine, on the opposite side of the Bay of Port Royal; also the City of St. Pierre.

The sister steamship, "Ville de Bordeaux," arriving from France on her way to Havana, afforded us the opportunity of returning to St. Thomas, where we spent ten days most delightfully among friends and descendants of friends after an absence of thirty-seven years. We reluctantly left in an English steamer for Havana, touching at St. Johns, Porto Rico, and arrived the 22d day of February. After spending a week at the New Hotel de la Pace, we em-

barked on the New Orleans steamer "Margaret" for Cedar
Keys, touching again at Key West, and had a fortunate
voyage back through the Gulf to the point of our departure, arriving on the 4th of March, to hear of the inaugura-
tion of President Hayes.

During our stay in Florida we went to Orange Lake, and
had a pleasant visit to Jennie Sampson's home at her husband's orange grove. On the lake I shot an alligator, and
had some good sport. We also made a trip up the Ockla-
waha River.

From Florida through Georgia we came to Washington,
where by invitation we spent an evening with Mrs. President Hayes at the White House. On our way home, stopping at New York, I was entertained by Judge Matsell at
his house until a late hour in the evening, which proved to
be our last meeting, as he died in July following. In June,
with Henry W. Hart, I went to Minnesota for the tenth
time, to show him the wonderful growth and progress of the
West, and my property in that flourishing State. July following, with mother and sister Ellen, we went to Saratoga.
Early in September our floor at No. 11 Beacon Street was
occupied by us.

The narrow-gauge Bedford and Billerica Railroad became embarrassed. It commenced running in November,
and went into bankruptcy next month. At this time we
associated ourselves with the Second Church, Robert Laird
Collier being its pastor. In February, 1878, George C.
Russell died. A general run on the savings banks began
about this time; I was then, as I am now, one of the trus-
tees of the Franklin. We left for Washington the last of
April for a visit there; and while at the Rig. House

received, May 10, a telegram announcing the death of
sister Harriet Ann. We returned immediately, and attended her funeral at North Reading. At Billerica we
entertained Captain Steele and his wife (Belle Faulkner),
previous to their departure for China. In June we again
went to Philadelphia, that my wife might consult Dr.
Mitchell and try the oxygen cure.

After our return home, at the solicitation of Mr. Collier,
our pastor, I concluded to go to Europe with him and visit
the Paris Exposition, with the intention of being absent
only five weeks. We left in the White-Star Steamer
"Celtic," and had a fine passage of eight and one half
days to Liverpool. Leaving Mr. Collier at the station in
London, I met by appointment Mrs. James Soden, who was
the daughter of Christian Dickmann of St. Thomas, my
sister's godchild, and who had lived with us when a child, at
West Cambridge. She had now a husband and a fine
grown-up family ; I had not seen her since she was twelve
years of age. I went directly to the Paris Exposition,
where I devoted most of a fortnight, and then returned
to London, where some days were spent with Mr. Soden
and his interesting family. I returned to New York in
the steamer "Germania," reaching home in Billerica a day
in advance of my expected arrival.

Soon after, we made a tour through the White Mountains, visiting Hattie Allen at Walpole and James Schouler
at Intervale. As a delegate I went to the Unitarian Conference at Saratoga. Samuel Hunt was killed by a fall in
his barn at Chelmsford, September 20. We took up our
winter quarters at Beacon Street, with mother. Thomas
Talbot was elected governor in November, and intelligence

of Belle Steele's death in China was received soon after.
Rheumatism had begun to trouble me again at intervals
during the winter.

We left, March 5, 1879, for Florida, and visited the principal cities on the river, and Tallahasse, where we met our
Nile friends, Mr. and Mrs. C. H. Lord. We then went to
Thomasville, Georgia, where we were detained by the rain
and floods several days, and finally had to go back again
into Florida, and return to Washington by Savannah and
Charleston. We met Ellen, who accompanied us home,
stopping at Philadelphia and New York. Soon after our
return we engaged an *appartement* of ten rooms at the
Hotel Bristol, then building, with a lease of five years, at a
rent of two thousand dollars per annum. We remained at
Beacon Street until July 24, when we took the Schouler-
Annex cottage, with sister Sarah, Emma, and Henry with
us. — Mr. John Wilson and family having the Schouler
cottage, and Mr. Tinkham the Bellevue. Joshua B. Holden
and family moved into the Pierce villa. We packed up our
numerous things at Beacon Street, and removed in October
to our new home at Hotel Bristol; previous to which we
made a visit to the new cottage of James Schouler at Intervale, and had a visit from our old friend John B. Russell,
with his daughter, who attended the Horticultural Society
dinner with me.

The concluding years of these biographical sketches
have but little general interest, and I give the common-
place events more in the form of a diary, from which I have
made these abstracts.

In April, 1880, the   of my niece, Emma
Haraden, to Capt. Jos.   my uncle, he having

VIEW OF THE JOSHUA BRITNELL HOMESTEAD.

returned some months previous from China. Mother, with Julia and Hattie Dorr, left the Bristol April 14; and the following day we closed up our rooms and went to Washington, I having a bad cough, and returned May 5 to the Bristol. On the 3d of June, Emma was married at Jamaica Plain. Soon after, Rev. E. A. Horton was installed pastor of our church. We went to Billerica, and June 16 visited Hattie Allen at Walpole. My cough continuing, I went alone, July 8, to Bethlehem, and home by Intervale.

On the 22d of July we opened the Schouler cottage for housekeeping, Captain Steele and Emma taking the Annex. I made an excursion to Mt. Desert to see Fannie Schouler and Mr. Williams, to whom she was under marriage engagement. With my wife and her sister I left, August 27, for Saratoga. The 17th of September was the great celebration of the anniversary of the city of Boston. On the 22d we went to Bellows Falls to attend the wedding of Fannie Schouler to James H. Williams, and from thence to Saratoga to the Unitarian Conference, — I as a delegate.

The Bennett Library Association had engaged my attention for some time, and my ground-plan for its building was adopted at a meeting October 15. On the 17th (my marriage anniversary) my beloved Aunt Ann Wilkins died at her niece's house, North Reading, and her remains were placed alongside of sister Harriet's in my lot in Mount Auburn. We resumed our housekeeping at the Bristol, October 26, with Julia and Hattie Dorr. Henry W. Hunt went to Chicago; was married there Feb. 10, 1881, and returned with his wife to Boston, where they lived during the winter and spring before going to housekeeping at Jamaica Plain.

In March I had another attack of rheumatism, and next month, when ready to start South, still another of an inflammatory nature, which delayed us. I was attended by Doctor Sumner, and had Frances Holt as nurse. We left with Hattie Dorr as my wife's maid for Washington, visiting as usual Philadelphia and New York to see our family connections. The summer was spent in Boston, Billerica, and Lynn. While visiting Joshua Holden, the great national excitement of the shooting of President Garfield took place, and the Fourth of July was an anxious one to us all. Another attack of rheumatism in my knee decided us to visit Alburg Springs in Vermont, as the St. Leon Springs in Canada had no accommodation for us. From there we went to Montreal, Plattsburg, and from Walpole home. The marriage of my nephew, John Schouler, to Hope Day, at Catskill, took place August 31: I attended alone, and from thence visited Richfield Springs for its baths, returning home by Saratoga, and visiting the two fairs in Boston, the Mechanics' and the New England. President Garfield died September 19. This month I was occupied in furnishing the Bennett Library. On the 10th of October we resumed housekeeping at the Bristol as usual for the winter. I attended at the Vendome the grand reception and ball given in honor of the French delegation to the Centennial of the Surrender of Cornwallis. The Bennett Library was dedicated October 24, a prominent part in the ceremony falling to me. On the 28th of December Aunt Mary McPherson died at the age of ninety-six.

March 11, 1882, with mother, Ellen, and my wife I attended the funeral of Mrs. Governor Armstrong, Beacon

VIEW OF THE BENNETT PUBLIC LIBRARY

Street, who was a cousin of my wife's father. We again left for Washington April 3, and visited John Schouler and wife at the Naval School, Annapolis; afterwards Philadelphia and New York, where my wife was ill some days at the Fifth Avenue Hotel. We returned home to the Bristol, and left there June 21 for Billerica. On the 28th I left for Minnesota, going thence to Castle Farm at Animosa, Iowa, where I had a pleasant visit with the Matsell family. After returning, July 16, we spent a week with Joshua B. Holden, Captain Steele and family occupying the Schouler cottage, and Mrs. Gregory, Alice and Sallie Haskell the Annex. August 31 we left Billerica for the mountains, visiting Fannie Williams, Hattie Allen, and James Schouler. My wife had a cold, and was ill during the whole trip of ten days through the mountains. Her illness continued a month at Billerica. On the 11th of October I went to the Bristol, where I had an attack of bronchitis. President Arthur arrived in Boston that day, and was escorted by the Ancient and Honorable Artillery Company to Marshfield. My wife recovered so as to join me on the 16th, and we were again domiciled for the winter.

Captain Steele and family, with sister Sarah, took a house in Philadelphia in October, where he was superintending the building of two steamers for the Oceanic Steam-Navigation Company of San Francisco. Mrs. Lander gave me a surprise in the location of her enlarged cottage on King Street. I joined the Unitarian Club at its formation; and the Unitarian Building Enterprise was started, in which I took an active part. Emily and James Schouler took a suite of rooms at the Bristol, and contributed to our home enjoyments. In February I revised

my "Nile Book" for publication by Lee & Shepard. This
month we were alarmed by the severe illness of sister
Sarah in Philadelphia, of pneumonia, and her son with a
nurse was despatched to her immediately.

We left again for the South March 12, in company with
Mrs. George Preston and daughter, and Hattie Dorr as
maid. After a week at Charleston, we all made a very pleasant tour of a month in Florida, returning to Fernandina,
where, parting with our friends, we took another month's
travel in Georgia and Tennessee, stopping on our way
home as usual in Washington, Philadelphia, and New
York, attending at Philadelphia the launch of the steamer
" Alameda," May 3, and arriving home on the 15th.

The summer of 1883 was spent in Boston, Billerica,
and Lynn, — including a month at Mrs. Page's, Ocean
Street, Lynn. I made a short visit to Bellows Falls and
Charlestown, N. H. Captain Steele's family, with Sarah,
returned from Philadelphia, and spent the summer in Lexington. July 20, with my wife and friends, we left for
Philadelphia, and from there enjoyed a very pleasant trial
trip on the " Alameda," with a large party, given by the
builders, Messrs. Cramp & Sons. Soon after, Captain
Steele took her to San Francisco, with his family and other
passengers, through the Straits of Magellan, in forty-five
days and fifteen hours running time, the shortest on record.
In the autumn the great drought gave us inconvenience in
Billerica. We visited Newport, to see John and Hope
Schouler, who were there a month.

The two exhibitions in Boston, the Foreign and American, attracted large numbers, most of whom passed the
Bristol. The visit of our corps, the Ancient and Honor-

able Artillery Company, to New York was quite an event
in its history, and I enjoyed it as a member without its
military duties or uniform. The political excitement against
Governor Butler had my strongest sympathy and co-opera-
tion. Pending the canvass, we resumed our winter housekeeping with our long-tried and capable domestics, mother
joining us at the end of October.

For the old church at Billerica I furnished a memorial
tablet to commemorate the sixty years of ministry of my
great-grandfather, Rev. Henry Cumings, D.D.

The great gubernatorial contest settled by the defeat
of Benjamin F. Butler by George D. Robinson (whose
acquaintance I made in Washington), gave me much satisfaction, as it did all lovers of decency and political hon-
esty in our State and beyond its borders.

Mrs. Dr. Wellington, of Arlington, died suddenly on the
18th of October, at the advanced age of 92 years. Her
husband was our old family physician.

Our old friend Miss Hannah P. Taylor came to Boston,
and went back to Pittsfield after staying a month. Joshua
B. Holden and his family left their Pierce Villa in Lynn
for the Riggs House, Washington, to spend the winter.

In November, the canvass for the election of Gen. A. P.
Martin as mayor, against Hugh O'Brien and the objection-
able partisan ring at City Hall, was a quiet but active one.
I was a delegate to both the Citizens' and Republican
conventions that nominated General Martin, having occasion at the same time to refuse a nomination for alderman
which was tendered to me. A very large vote was cast at
the election, which resulted in the choice of General Martin,
and in a great triumph for those citizens who favored a

good and honest city government, without distinction of party. General Martin I first met in the South, on a railroad train, when with his undressed wound received in battle he was on his way home. Finding him nearly fainting from fatigue, I gave him a restorative, — an act he has always remembered and often spoken of.

The great drought still continued in December, causing great inconvenience from dry wells in the country. The Foreign Exhibition continued open during the month. Mrs. Dr. Stephen Ball returned from one of her extensive travelling tours in Europe. Captain Steele and his family came back by rail from California, there being no more steamers to build under his superintendence, and at the end of the year there was a happy reunion at Jamaica Plain.

The declining sun of the year, which had promised to give us a golden setting and a happy termination to this life-record of events, was suddenly clouded over, and set amidst grief in our family circle, by the sudden death, Dec. 29, of NELLIE, eldest daughter of George and Fannie Tinkham, at the age of eleven years, and the critical condition (at the present writing) of the youngest daughter. The scourge of scarlet fever invaded the happy household just before Christmas, striking down within a week all four of the children. Nellie passed away on the third day of the attack. She had a very attractive and sweet disposition, and a bright intellect.

We wait and hope.

In closing this brief narrative of the principal events of my life on the verge of "three score years and ten," I will state that I have now more occupations than I desire, and it may not be out of place to enumerate them. Besides having the care of my own property and that of my wife and her mother (the real estate of the heirs of Joshua Bennett being yet undivided), I am a trustee of the estate of Stephen Ball, of the Washingtonian Home, and the Franklin Savings Bank. I am also an active member of the Second Church, of Columbian Lodge of Free and Accepted Masons, of the Ancient and Honorable Artillery Company, the Art Club, the Unitarian Club, the New England Historic Genealogical Society, the Bostonian Society, the Memorial Association, the Bunker-Hill Monument Association, and the South-End Industrial School. In addition to all this, I am interested in many charitable societies in the city. In my business labors, however, I am most ably assisted by my nephew, Henry W. Hart, whose long experience and familiarity with my whole business, together with his fidelity and trustworthiness, render my executive labor comparatively easy.

Finally, I wish to express here my gratitude to an all-wise, beneficent, and overruling Deity for His many blessings, among which I have learned to appreciate health as one of the most desirable and valuable.

WILLIAM WILKINS WARREN.

Boston, Hotel Bristol,
Jan. 1, 1884.

Kennard, William B. Kennard, D. Webster Ring,
C. H. Lord, Charles G. Laurat, Nathan Morse, S.
W. Richardson, Rev. James Reed, J. M. Ebenmachs, D. W. Russell, Alexander H. Rice, Hon. A.
A. Ranney, James Schouler, Commander John
Schouler, U. S. N., Rev. William Schouler, Charles
Terry, Dr. Talbot, Chas. G. Wood, Henry Walker,
Alexander Wadsworth, Augustus Whittemore,

The bridesmaid and groomsman, Mrs. S. W.
Hart and Mr. E. B. Smith, respectively, who officiated in those capacities at the wedding fifty
years ago, were also present. The ushers were
Messrs. Spencer W. Richardson, William H. Kennard and Charles G. Wood. Mrs. Warren's mother,
Mrs. Joshua Bennet, who has now reached the
advanced age of ninety-three, was present, a remarkable example of well-preserved old age. The
exercises included poems by Rev. E. A. Horton,
Rev. M. J. Savage, and Elijah B. Smith of West
Medford. There were, also, poems contributed
by Rev. M. G. Allen and Rev. James Reed, which
were not read on account of want of time. The
reception lasted from seven to ten o'clock, P. M.,
and was entirely informal and social in its character. The floral decorations were superb, comprising plants, cut flowers and set pieces in great
profusion and variety. Music was furnished during the evening by the Germania Orchestra, and
an elegant collation was served. The reception
was a most successful one, and was an occasion
much enjoyed by the host, the hostess and their
numerous guests. The following is the poem contributed and read by Rev. E. A. Horton:

LINES FOR MR. AND MRS. W. W. WARREN.

"No gifts desired," the cards say
    That summon us tonight;
But surely there are some things
    You 'll not decline at sight.

We bring you smiling faces
    And hearty shakes of hand,
With sundry jokes and stories,
    As much as you can stand.

We bring congratulations
    Most rosy, yet most true;
And add some cogitations
    Quite wholesome, if not new.

And now, with all these presents,
    I offer you some rhymes;
I wish they were much brighter,
    In keeping with these times.

But poets are not made, you know—
    In fact, I find them scarce;
For lack of better stanzas
    I hope you 'll let these pass.

I want to ask some questions,
    And state a fact or two;
So, for such simple service,
    These limping lines may do.

To give our repetitions
    As we greet you o'er and o'er;
I know felicitations
    Become at last a bore.

But as you have lived fifty,
    Yes, fifty years as one,
You must expect the people
    Will ask how it was done.

Pray gratify the curious
    And tell the story out,
Let others know the secret,—
    They 'll practise it no doubt.

Just tell how through the changes
    Of fifty wedded years
You kept so young and hearty,
    For so the fact appears.

How have you found the journey?
    Just as your fancy hoped?
Have all the paths been verdant,
    Each highway gently sloped?

Have larks sung in the ether
    And hedgerows bloomed with flowers?
Has romance stood before you
    And sided life and it's hours?

Ah, no! stern circumstances oft conduct,
    And sad . . . . . .
. . . .
    . . . .

... ...
But he is best from many
Who has a trusty wife.

As I have scanned your names, my friends,
This met I plainly see,
It took a B to W,
Then you must couple B.

This is the secret, surely,
The fifty years proclaim;
A partnership most hearty,
A doubled life and name.

Together, runs the motto,
Our noblest work is done;
"Together" is the secret
By which the world is won.

By choral power of union
Life's great reforms are sung;
By pulling all together
Hope's mighty bells are rung.

What steamers cross the ocean,
Cunarders, White Star, all!
But for freight the Warren line
Excels the so great and small.

Three cheers, then, for the Warren line,
That sails o'er time so well!
May prosperous winds and kindly skies
A happy future tell!

The Bennet name we honor, too;
It stands for kindly deeds;
Their benefactions many
Shine out o'er human needs.

To her, serene and happy,
Who bears old age along,
As Autumn wears her beauty,
Or reapers sing their song;

Who watched her child as infant,
As bride, as faithful wife,
Who spans, wellnigh in prospect,
A century of life;

To her whose heart so tender
Beats kindly for her race,
Whose calm and constant goodness
Is mirrored in her face;

To her we bring glad greetings,
With messages of love;
May many years retain thee
E'er thou shalt dwell above!

'T is worth our while in passing
This striking note to make—
The Holdens are Hold-outs, you see—
Hold on! I 've made mistake.

They are good Hold-fast people,
To ties and memories true,
But from their hold of doing
Hold-back they never do.

The Old World you have traversed,
In tropic regions dwelt,
But ever for your country here
The love that patriots felt.

Upon the Nile you've floated,
O'er Alpine glaciers crept;
Mused in the Colosseum,
'Neath Antwerp's soft climes slept.

Yet ever fondly turning
To native soil and shore,
Your hearts grow warm with ardor
To welcome home once more.

Then gather, freely gather,
O memory, in thy hands,
The sparkling scenes of pleasure,
Enjoyed through many lands.

Settle this puzzling statement
And I shall be right glad—
The house of Warren, Boston,
No war-ring ways has had.

'T is true our friend goes fighting,
When the "Ancients" take the field,
But we never hear of bullets
Or of peaceful blood congealed.

Dear friends, beneath all jesting
Our serious thoughts has away;
We wish you, here ... ...,
Fresh joy ... ...

We wish you a ... ...
In heart ... ...
And ... ...
With ... ...

We w ... ...
S ... ...
And ... ...
That ... ...

The fifty ... ...
The ... ...
The ... ...
Bel ... ...

S ... ...
T ... ...
A ... ...
W ... ...

GENEALOGIES.

———◆———

THE GENEALOGY OF WILLIAM WILKINS WARREN, IN-
CLUDING THAT OF THE FAMILIES CONNECTED BY
BLOOD OR MARRIAGE, — NAMELY: BENNETT, SCHOU-
LER, RUSSELL, CUMINGS, WILKINS, CHEEVER, AND
HUNT.

T has been claimed that the Warrens of Great
Britain and elsewhere are the descendants of
William de Warrenne, Earl of Surrey, born in
England 1087. However that may be, the
paternal ancestor of the subject of the following gene-
alogy was born in England in 1585, and emigrated to
America, according to "Bond's History of Watertown,
Mass.," as follows : —

WILLIAM WILKINS WARREN FAMILY.

1. *JOHN WARREN came to America with his four children, in
1630, and settled in Watertown, and from 1636 to 1640
was a Selectman there. He owned 188 acres of land. In
1654 he was fined for not attending public worship. — 1 1

* This indicates the lineal descent.

Sabbaths, 5s. each, £3 10s. ; and his house was searched for Quakers, etc. This shows he was not a rigid conformist to Puritan ideas then prevailing.

His four children were *John, Mary, Daniel*, and *Elizabeth*.

2. *JOHN had by marriage 2 sons — *John, Samuel* — and 5 daughters.

DANIEL had 3 sons — *Daniel, John, Joshua* — and 7 daughters.

3. JOHN had 3 sons — *John, Jonathan*, and *Daniel*.

DANIEL had 3 sons — *Daniel, Jonas 1st, Jonas 2d* — and 7 daughters.

JOSHUA had 3 sons — *Joshua, Nathaniel, Daniel* — and 8 daughters.

*JOHN, of Weston, had 6 sons — *John, Samuel, Thomas, David, Benjamin, William* — and 4 daughters.

SAMUEL had 3 sons — *Samuel, Nathan, John* — and 4 daughters.

4. DANIEL m. GARFIELD for 2d wife ; had 4 sons — *Samuel, Daniel, Asa, Elijah* — and 5 daughters.

*Dea. JOHN, of Weston, had 3 wives and 6 sons — *John, Josiah, Isaac, *Elisha, Ebenezer, Abijah* — and 7 daughters.

JONATHAN, of Weston, had 12 daughters, no sons.

5. JOHN, Jr., of Weston, had 2 wives and 9 sons — *Jonathan, John 1st, John 2d, Jonathan, Jedediah, Philemon, Silas, Ezra, James* — and 8 daughters.

JOSIAH, of Weston, had 4 sons — *Abijah, Josiah, Isaac, John* — and 5 daughters.

*ELISHA, of Weston, married SARAH ABBOTT, daughter of Nehemiah ; and had 6 sons — *Nehemiah, Amos, Micah, Abijah, Isaac, Nathan* — and 3 daughters. (Isaac was the father of the late Judge George Washington Warren).

6. *AMOS (grandfather of William Wilkins) was born Oct. 22, 1748, and married ELIZABETH WHITTEMORE, Nov. 25, 1773. He lived in West Cambridge ; was a cordwainer. His wife Elizabeth was daughter of Samuel Whittemore and his wife Love Stone. Samuel was son of the famous Captain Samuel, who, over 80 years of age, distinguished

himself on the retreat of the British from Lexington, April 19, 1775. AMOS was a precinct committee-man and assessor, 1784-85. In the early part of the present century he purchased a farm in West Medford, where he died in 1831. The farm near the depot, on the side of a hill, is now laid out into streets, one of which bears his name.

His surviving widow, who was born Oct. 20, 1753, died May 31, 1842, aged 89 years, at the residence of her son-in-law, Col. Thomas Russell, where she had made it her home during her widowhood.

The children of AMOS and ELIZABETH were —

1. *Elizabeth*, born Aug. 29, 1774, who died in 1775.
2. *Elizabeth*, born June 22, 1777 ; married *Col. Thomas Russell*, of West Cambridge, Dec. 21, 1800, who died March 31, 1866. *Elizabeth* died Feb. 9, 1845, aged 68 years. (See *Russell family*.)
3. AMOS, born June 22, 1779 ; married Susan Frost, Dec. 10, 1802, and had two children, Eliza and Susan. (See *Hunt family*.)
4. ISAAC (father of William Wilkins Warren) was born in West Cambridge, April 22, 1787. Married FRANCES WILKINS, daughter of Dr. William Wilkins, and grand-daughter of Rev. Henry Cumings, D.D., of Billerica, May 27, 1811. (See *Cumings family*.)
5. SARAH ABBOTT, born 1790. Married to REUBEN JOHNSON, May 20, 1810. She died April 29, 1811, aged 21, and her infant died May 11, following. *Reuben* married *Rachel Buckman*, Oct. 24, 1826. Their daughter *Sarah Ann* was born in 1827, and two other children who died young. *Sarah Ann* married *Mr. Dunckley*, of Boston, now settled in the West.
6. ELISHA, born 1794 : died in 1795.

The children of ISAAC and FRANCES, all born in West Cambridge, were —

1. *Harriet Ann*, born Sept. 30, 1812.
2. *William Wilkins*, born April 11, 1814.

7

3. *Frances Eliza*, born Jan. 10, 1816.

4. *Sarah Johnson*, born Feb. 2, 1818.

ISAAC went to New York about 1820. and remained away
until about 1840, when he revisited West Cambridge, returned to New York, and was never heard from afterwards.

FRANCES, his wife, joined the church in Medford about
1822, when she and her children were baptized by the
venerable Dr. Osgood, at the Unitarian church. She was
married, in May, 1826, to CAPTAIN JOSEPH ATTWOOD, of
the merchant marine service. In November of same year
Captain Attwood, with his wife and her son-in-law, Russell
Smith, and Harriet Ann, his wife, sailed for St. Thomas,
W. I., to take up their residence there. Mr. Smith had
been married but a short time previous, to Harriet Ann
Warren. Mrs. FRANCES ATTWOOD died in St. Thomas of
yellow fever, Jan. 28, 1827, aged 35. CAPTAIN ATTWOOD
returned home soon after, and died in June, 1827.

1. HARRIET ANN was married to RUSSELL SMITH, a jeweller in
Boston (whose father, Pardon Smith, lived in Tiverton,
R. I.), by the Rev. "Father" Ballou, in the autumn of
1826. She was his second wife. They lived in St.
Thomas twelve years, where Mr. Smith built a finely
situated house overlooking the city. In 1830 they were
joined by *William Wilkins Warren*, and in 1837 by himself and wife. HARRIET ANN went with her husband on a
visit to Boston in the Spring of 1838, where he died
Oct. 18 following. HARRIET ANN married GEORGE M.
CHALWILL, of St. Thomas, at Arlington, in September,
1840. He was of English parents, and born in the island
of Tortola, adjacent to St. Thomas. He died in San
Francisco, Cal., in 1847. She returned from there soon
after, lived in Boston, afterwards in Billerica and North
Reading, and died at the latter place, May 9, 1878.

2. WILLIAM WILKINS married REBECCA BENNETT, of Billerica,
Oct. 17, 1837. She was the second daughter of *Joshua
Bennett* and his wife *Eleanor*, and was born in Boston,

MRS SARAH J HART

June 18, 1819. Mr. Warren, with his wife, embarked for his home in the island of St. Thomas, in November, 1837, and visited the United States in 1839, and finally left St. Thomas and returned to Boston in May, 1840. (See *Biography of William Wilkins Warren, and Genealogy of Bennett family.*)

3. FRANCES ELIZA was married to WILLIAM SCHOULER, son of *James* and *Margaret Schouler*, of West Cambridge (Arlington), in that town, Oct. 6, 1835. *William Schouler* was born at Kilbarchan, Scotland, Dec. 31, 1814, and came with his parents to this country at an early age. GENERAL WILLIAM SCHOULER'S career as an accomplished writer, journalist, author, legislator, and efficient Adjutant-General during the great Rebellion is well known. He had the entire confidence of Governor Andrew, and succeeded in gaining the hearts of all who knew him. The beautiful monument over his remains at Forest Hills Cemetery memorializes and attests his worth. He died at Jamaica Plain, Oct. 24, 1872. FRANCES, his wife, died while visiting one of her sons at Syracuse, N. Y., Nov. 1, 1874. Their children were *Harriet Ann*, born in West Cambridge, June 14, 1837; *James*, born in West Cambridge, March 20, 1839; *William*, born in West Cambridge, Feb. 25, 1841; *Frances*, born in Lowell and died soon after; *John*, born in Lowell, Nov. 30, 1846; *Fanny*, born in Boston, Jan. 10, 1852. (See *Schouler family*.)

4. SARAH JOHNSON married OLIVER W. BLAKE in West Cambridge, Aug. 16, 1842, who died Oct. 12, 1848. Their children were: *Frances Warren*, who died in 1844, one year old; *Emma Frances*, born Oct. 16, 1845, and *George*, who died aged 10 months. SARAH married HENRY HART, of Boston, Dec. 5, 1850, — who was born Oct. 18, 1818, and died Jan. 31, 1856.

EMMA FRANCES married EBEN C. HARADEN in Boston, Sept. 5, 1867. He died March 13, 1872. She married CAPTAIN JOSEPH STEELE, of China, at Jamaica Plain,

June 3, 1880. Their children were: *Joseph Vernon Steele*,
born at Jamaica Plain, July 2, 1881 ; *Sarah Warren*, born
in Lynn, July 26, 1882.

The only child of SARAH JOHNSON WARREN by her
marriage with *Henry Hart*, was HENRY WARREN HART,
born in Boston, Dec. 30, 1851. He married at Chicago,
Feb. 10, 1881, NELLIE SUSAN ANDRUS, born at Council
Bluffs, Iowa, Nov. 26, 1857. Her father, William Cone
Andrus, married Laura P. Paine. The child of HENRY
and NELLIE (1883), *Henry Warren Hart, Jr.*, was born at
Jamaica Plain, Oct. 7, 1881.

BENNETT FAMILY.[1]

JAMES BENNETT, of Groton, of Scotch descent, was born in
1704. His son, MOSES BENNETT, born Dec. 5, 1736, married
ANNA BLANCHARD. Their children were five sons, — *Stephen*,
James, Jonathan, Thomas, and *Joseph*. The first two settled
in Billerica, near the Burlington line, and paid taxes in 1780.
JAMES BENNETT (grandfather of Rebecca, wife of William
Wilkins Warren), was born in Groton, March 29, 1758, and
married MARY WALKER, of Charlestown, April 13, 1780.
She was born Dec. 9, 1758, and died in 1857. Their children
were *James*, born Sept. 2, 1780; *Edward*, born May 29, 1782 ;
Mary, born July 11, 1785 ; *Joshua*, born Nov. 24, 1792 ;
John, born June 15, 1794 ; *Nancy*, born Aug. 13, 1798 ;
Lucy, born Sept. 19, 1800.

JOSHUA married ELEANOR RICHARDSON, daughter of Ebenezer
Richardson, Jr., of Medford, and his wife, Susan Tufts, Oct. 8,
1815. Ebenezer had three wives and ten children : namely,
Joel, Rebecca, Nathaniel, Isaac, Susan, Lucy, Martha, Mary,
ELEANOR, and Lucretia. The father of Ebenezer, Jr., had
seven wives and five children. The children of JOSHUA and

---

[1] See Hazen's History of Billerica, 1883.

MRS. ELEANOR BENNETT

ELEANOR were ELLEN, born Feb. 15, 1816; and REBECCA, born June 18, 1819. (See *Warren family.*)

ELLEN married GEORGE HOLDEN, of Billerica, April 27, 1841. who was born June 10, 1802, and died Feb. 6, 1876. (See "Hazen's History of Billerica.") The children of ELLEN and GEORGE were *Ellen Bennett,* born Dec. 27, 1841, died Sept. 22, 1848; *Rebecca Bennett,* born Aug. 16, 1843, died Aug. 17, 1875; *Frances Ann,* born April 4, 1845; *Joshua Bennett,* born March 5, 1850. FRANCES ANN married GEORGE H. TINKHAM, of Boston (who was born in Boston, Oct. 11, 1834), Sept. 19, 1869. Their children were: *George Holden,* born Oct. 29, 1870; *Ellen Bennett,* born March 12, 1872, died Dec. 29, 1883; *Rebecca Warren,* born Aug. 11, 1873; *Eleanor Frances,* born Sept. 23, 1875. JOSHUA married IDA L. MOULTON, of Laconia, N.H., who was born June 4, 1850. Their children were: *Annie Ellen,* born April 2, 1873; *Mary Bennett,* born Sept. 25, 1874; *Josina Bennett,* born Dec. 20, 1876; *Natalie Frances,* Feb. 26, 1880.

REBECCA, second daughter of *Joshua* and *Eleanor,* married WILLIAM WILKINS WARREN, in Billerica, Oct. 17, 1837, and went to his home in the island of St. Thomas, W. I. They had no children. (See his *Autobiography.*)

SCHOULER FAMILY.

THE children of JAMES and MARGARET SCHOULER, of Kilbarchan, Scotland, were *John, Robert, William, Janet, Eliza,* and *James,* all of whom were married. Three sons were born in Scotland, the two daughters and youngest son in the United States.

WILLIAM married FRANCES ELIZA WARREN, Oct. 6, 1835. (See *Warren family.*) Their five children, whose births are already recorded elsewhere, were all married as follows: HARRIET ANN married REV. NATHANIEL GLOVER ALLEN, of

Boston, January 27, 1875. Their children were: *Leslie*, born
July 18, 1876; *Glover*, born Feb. 8, 1879, and *Janet Warren*,
born Feb. 9, 1882. JAMES married EMILY FULLER COCHRAN,
of Boston, Dec. 14. 1870. WILLIAM married SOPHIE BRAINE
HEATON, of Brooklyn, N.Y., April 20, 1871. Their children
were: *Alice Heaton*, born Oct. 9, 1872; *William*, born Nov.
6, 1873, died Nov. 20, 1874; *Frances Warren*, born March 3,
1876. JOHN married HOPE DAY, of Catskill, N. Y., Aug. 31,
1881. FANNY WILKINS married JAMES HENRY WILLIAMS,
Jr., of Bellows Falls, Vt., Sept. 20, 1880. Their child, *Margaret Schouler*, was born March 20, 1882.

RUSSELL FAMILY.

ELIZABETH WARREN, daughter of Amos (aunt to William Wilkins Warren), married THOMAS RUSSELL, of West Cambridge,
Dec. 21, 1800. His father, of the same name. was the son
of Jason Russell and Anna Whittemore, who had two sons,
Thomas and Aaron, and two daughters. The latter and
Aaron died young. The survivor, THOMAS, born Nov. 23,
1776, commanded a regiment of cavalry raised during the
War of 1812, and he served many years in the State Legis-
lature, and in the most important of town offices. He was
much esteemed for his genial and gentle disposition, his
kindness shown to all; a prudent counsellor, honest and
fair in his dealings, frugal and temperate in his habits. His
wife ELIZABETH, many years an invalid, died Feb. 9, 1845,
aged 68 years. He died March 30, 1866, a fine specimen, in
physique and appearance, of an old gentleman, in the 90th
year of his age. The old corner grocery-store which his
father and himself kept, has continued in the hands of his
son and grandson to the present time 1883, where may be
found the fifth generation of the family engaged in the same
business, continued under the same roof over a century.

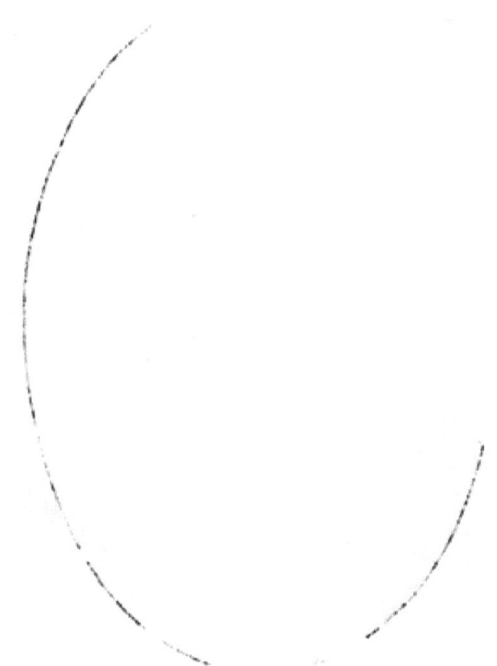

GENERAL WILLIAM SCHOULER.

MRS. WILLIAM SCHOULER

The children of Col. THOMAS RUSSELL and his wife
ELIZABETH were: *Thomas Jefferson*, born Dec. 10, 1801.
Eliza Ann, born March 29, 1803, died single — an invalid
for many years — Aug. 28, 1864. *George Clinton*, born Feb.
4, 1805, died Feb. 15, 1878. *Mary Jane*, born May 17, 1806,
died single, June 7, 1827. THOMAS JEFFERSON was married
to *Mary Locke Perry*, April 8, 1830. Their children were:
Thomas Henry, born Feb. 3, 1831; *William Warren*, born
Sept. 7, 1833; *Mary Jane*, born Aug. 9, 1845. THOMAS
HENRY married *Harriet A. Teel*, Aug. 22, 1851. Their children were: *Frederick Henry*, born May 11, 1853; *Alice
Maria* was born March 18, 1856. FREDERICK HENRY married *Josephine Odion*, Sept. 21, 1881. WILLIAM WARREN
married *Lydia W. Locke*, Dec. 17, 1860; he died childless at
St. Augustine, Fla., June 9, 1876. MARY JANE married
Frank G. Sampson, of New Orleans, Sept. 21, 1871. Their
child, *Olive H.* was born June 5, 1876. GEORGE CLINTON
married *Sophronia Fessenden*, May 23, 1830. Their children
were: *Mary Eliza*, born May 4, 1831, died Sept. 16, 1841;
Harriet Ann, born May 13, 1833, died same day; *Harriet
Ann, 2d*, born Sept. 22, 1834; *George Harris*, born Dec. 30,
1836, died July 18, 1856; *Ellen Sophronia*, born Feb. 4, 1839;
Francis Fessenden, born June 28, 1841; *Mary Eliza*, born
Oct. 14, 1843; *Caroline Rebecca*, born Dec. 19, 1845, died
Dec. 7, 1861; *Charles Warren*, born May 30, 1850, died Sept.
26, 1852. *Harriet Ann* married *Charles Fessenden*, Nov. 25,
1858, and had no children. *Ellen Sophronia* married *Samuel
Payson Prentiss*, Dec. 27, 1860, and had no children. *Francis
Fessenden* married *Clara Louisa Blake*, Dec. 29, 1863. Their
children were: *George Otis*, born Dec. 4, 1864; *Nellie
Louise*, born Aug. 2, 1866; *Isabella Blake*, born Oct. 2,
1868; *Annie Frances*, born Dec. 6, 1878, died March 17,
1881.

JOHN CUMINGS, of Rowley, Mass., married SARAH HOWLETT, of Ipswich, 1667. He removed to Dunstable, and was one of the leading men there. Their children were six sons and one daughter. He died Dec. 1, 1700, and his wife Dec. 7. Their son *John* had seven children, of whom *Samuel* was born Oct. 6, 1680, and lived in Groton, where his son *Jerahmael* was born Oct. 10, 1711, and married *Hannah Farwell*. He had three daughters and two sons, *Henry* and *Jotham;* and died Oct. 21, 1747. The latter has left a numerous posterity in Plymouth.

HENRY CUMINGS was born Sept. 16, 1739 ; graduated at Harvard College, 1760 ; taught school in Reading, 1761 ; studied theology with Daniel Emerson, in Hollis ; was ordained in Billerica, Jan. 26, 1763, and died Sept. 5, 1823, in office. The Rev. Mr. Whitman was his colleague from 1814 to 1823. Harvard College gave him the honorary degree of D.D. in 1800. He was often called in council, and to preach on public occasions. There are seventeen of his printed publications, revised by himself for Mr. Farmer's Historical Memoir. He married, May 19, 1763, ANN LAMBERT, of Reading, who died Jan. 5, 1784. He married her sister, Mrs. MARGARET BRIGGS, Nov. 14, 1786, who died June 2, 1790. He married his third wife, Sept. 20, 1791, SARAH BRIDGE, daughter of Rev. Ebenezer Bridge, of Chelmsford, born July 25, 1742, died Feb. 25, 1812. His five children by his first wife were : *Ann*, born July 31, 1768, not married ; *Farnes*, born April 7, 1770 ; *Elizabeth*, born Aug. 15, 1772, married *Lewis Gould*, no children ; *Henry*, born Sept. 9, 1774, graduated at Harvard College, died unmarried, near Louisville, Ky., 1828 ; *John*, born Feb. 11, 1781, married and had two daughters ; FRANCES (grandmother of William Wilkins Warren), married Dr. WILLIAM WILKINS.

Henry Cumings

Copy from the Tombstone Inscription in the old burialground of Billerica.

"Beneath this stone rest the remains of the Rev. Henry Cummings, D.D., late pastor of the Church and Christian Society in Billerica. Born Sept. 25, 1739. Ordained, Jan. 25, 1763. Died, Sept. 5, 1823.

"Possessing intellectual powers of the highest order, he was eminently learned, pious, and faithful; and by his life and example illustrated and recommended the doctrines and virtues he taught and inculcated. In grateful remembrance of his distinguished virtue, this stone is erected by the people of his charge."

Much valuable information of the life of Dr. Cumings can be had from "Hazen's History of Billerica," published 1883, from which the Cumings genealogy in part has been taken.

WILKINS FAMILY.

TIMOTHY WILKINS, of Middletown, bought a farm of 112 acres, in 1739. Married MARGARET MUNROE, and had two sons, *William* and *Isaac.*

WILLIAM (grandfather of William Wilkins Warren) was born April 1, 1765. Married May 10, 1789, FRANCES, daughter of the Rev. HENRY CUMINGS, D.D. He removed to Marblehead in 1807, and died May 7, 1811, aged 46. His children were: *Frances*, born Feb. 18, 1790, and *Frances* 2d, born March 4, 1791; married ISAAC WARREN, of N. Cambridge, May 27, 1811. They were the parents of William Wilkins Warren. (See *Warren family.*) HENRIETTA, born Feb. 18, 1793, married Feb. 5, 1827, ... CHEEVER, of Andover. (See *Cheever family.*) ANN, July 8, 1795; died single, Oct. 17, 1880. WILLIAM, July 4, 1797; married and had two children, in Louisville, Ky. HENRY CUMINGS, born Nov. 5, 1801; married and died in the West. SIDNEY LAM, born ... 22, 1803; died in the West. AUGUSTUS, born March 21, 1807; died single in Billerica. Aged ... *Isaac*, brother of Dr. William Wilkins, was born in Brownsville, Me.; was married and had two ...

CHEEVER FAMILY.

HENRIETTA WILKINS married as aforesaid *James Cheever*. Their children were —

1. HENRIETTA, born May 27, 1827. Married CAPTAIN WINSLOW L. KNOWLES, March 17, 1859, who died in Calcutta, Oct. 5, 1863, and his executor was William Wilkins Warren. Their only child, *Winslow Lewis*, was born Feb. 8, 1861.

2. FRANCES ANN, born in Andover, Aug. 15, 1830. Married JOSEPH ELBRIDGE HOLT, at Reading, Dec. 28, 1849, who was born July 27, 1828, and died Aug. 25, 1882. Their children were: *Emma Frances*, born Oct. 24, 1850; *Henrietta Cheever*, July 18, 1852; *Mary Carter*, Jan. 28, 1858; *Ann Wilkins*, July 22, 1860; *James Osgood*, March 28, 1867. Mary, died Oct. 22, 1862. Henrietta died Sept. 14, 1877.

3. JAMES OSGOOD, born Dec. 25, 1833, and married, Sept. 27, 1883, SOPHIA AUGUSTA PRENTICE, of Boston.

4. WILLIAM WILKINS, born June 30, 1835; married JENNIE BLOOD, of Sterling, June 11, 1867, who was born Oct. 14, 1839.

HUNT FAMILY.

1. ELIZA WARREN, daughter of *Amos Warren* (see *Warren family*), born Sept. 18, 1803, married SAMUEL C. HUNT (son of Joshua Hunt, of Tewksbury) April 4, 1824. He was born June 28, 1797, and died from a fall, Sept. 29, 1878. Their children were: *Samuel Chamberlain*, born Sept. 6, 1825; *George Warren*, born March 5, 1827; *Ann Eliza*, born May 1, 1828; *William Warren*, born Dec. 5, 1829; *Olive Chamberlain*, born March 10, 1832; *Hannah Chamberlain*, born Aug. 19, 1834; *John Henry*,

born April 20, 1836; *Sarah Julia* and *Susan Barron*, twins, Sept. 3, 1839; *Henry Brown*, Oct. 29, 1847.

SAMUEL C. married *Sarah K. Gardner*, July 10, 1848. Their children were: *William Barron*, born Oct. 30, 1849, died Feb. 19, 1864; *Frank Albert*, born July 10, 1852; *Anna Warren*, born Dec. 8, 1853, died April 11, 1861; *Eliza Peters*, born June 11, 1855; *William Chamberlain*, born Dec. 20, 1856; *Olive Chamberlain*, born June 21, 1860. GEORGE W. married *Ellen C. Parkhurst*, Aug. 10. 1857. Their children were: *George William*, born June 26, 1858; *Edson Parkhurst*, born July ———, died Jan. 28, 1873; *Charles Warren*, born July 24, 1866; *Elizabeth Abbott* and *John Parkhurst* both died. WILLIAM BARRON married, in California, *Madame Dumas*. Their children were: *William Eugene*, born Sept. 29, 1862; *William Broderick*, born July 28, 1864; *Elizabeth Abbott Warren*, born Dec. 14, 1865. JOHN HENRY married and had: *Edwin F. Gay*, born Oct. 9, 1866; *John Horsford*, born March 19, 1868; *Eugenia*, born Oct. 23, 1869; *Walter*, born May 12, 1872; *Richard*, born Oct. 20, 1877. SARAH JULIA married *John H. Loring*. Their children were: *Susan Frances*, born Oct. 9, 1866; *Jane Burbank*, born June 28, 1869; *Alfred Orlando*, born March 20, 1871; *Benjamin Chamberlain*, born Aug. 30, 1876. *Earnest John* and *Levi Howard*, dates of births not obtained. The other daughters now living are unmarried.

2. SUSAN WARREN, daughter of *Amos*, married *John Buckman*, of Lynn, and had 2 sons, *Warren* and *George*. The latter was killed at Gettysburg, in a New Hampshire regiment. *Warren* is a printer in the "Daily Advertiser" office (1882). SUSAN died Dec. 10, 1879.